Books by Samuel Shellabarger

BIOGRAPHY

THE CHEVALIER BAYARD

LORD CHESTERFIELD AND HIS WORLD

FICTION

THE BLACK GALE

CAPTAIN FROM CASTILE

PRINCE OF FOXES

THE KING'S CAVALIER

LORD VANITY

THE TOKEN

The Token

The Token

by

SAMUEL SHELLABARGER

ILLUSTRATED BY STEELE SAVAGE

LITTLE, BROWN AND COMPANY

Boston · Toronto

Published simultaneously in Canada
by Little, Brown & Company (Canada) Limited

PRINTED IN THE UNITED STATES OF AMERICA

Contents

The Token

The Silver Girdle

ERVAIS, the abbot, waited on Lord Stephen, who was called the Wolf, in his castle of Sarzeau. This Stephen was a man of good family, for he was son of Stephen Broadaxe, the son of Eric, an earl from the North who had come down with long ships by the coast, and won lands for himself. Stephen was of great courage and of a strength more than human, so that men wondered at it. He was short of speech, but just in his dealings. He had a red beard and eyes like a wolf's.

Abbot Gervais had come on the part of Count Raoul of Roche-Bernard to learn if marriage could be brought about between the count and

The Token

Lady Blanche, Stephen's daughter, for it was known that the wide manor of Seaubois would follow her in dowry. The abbot spoke fully on this matter, showing that good would come both to Sarzeau and Roche-Bernard from the bargain.

The two sat alone, and my Lord Stephen answered little, only hacking at the table before him with his knife. When the abbot ended, he said they must ask counsel of his son in this affair, and sent forth to fetch in Lady Blanche's eldest brother, John of Sarzeau. He was an upstanding, silent man like his father, good both in war and peace. When the offer of Count Raoul was made known to him, he answered after a time that he thought well of it, as there was much to gain from the friendship of Count Raoul and his kin.

Then Lord Stephen put the knife back in its sheath and said: "Holy father, I am of equal mind with my son, yet loath I am to grant your asking. God has favored me in life. I have added to the lands of my father and grandsire; I have had strength of body; three sons are mine, who will increase our holdings after me. But this is not all. My good wife, dying, left in her stead this daughter, who is dear to me. She is wise and bold, rides well, and has fair hair, befitting our blood, and gray eyes that please me. Twenty years have I loved her, and when she is gone little will there be to cherish in Sarzeau." Lord Stephen walked up and down, and twisted his beard between his fingers. "But I love her, and this is woman's talk. Let her live free of me. Say then to Count Raoul that he come hither, and if he find favor with her, it shall be according to his wish."

When Abbot Gervais carried back these tidings to Roche-Bernard, it was said that Count Raoul laughed because so weighty a matter should hang upon the liking of a girl.

Count Raoul was a tall and handsome man with hair that curled on his shoulders. He had a ready tongue and courtly manners with women. He was much loved by them, but men cared less for him. He was brave and skilled in arms, yet he praised himself overmuch.

He now made rich provision in dress and equipment for his wooing at Sarzeau—more than his purse warranted: the best of horses, ermine and velvet, gold chains and new armor. Thus he set forward in Maytime with his men. A goodlier company could not be found in the land. And Lord Stephen, on his part, when he heard of their coming, rode out to meet them with his sons.

When they reached the castle, and Stephen Wolf had drunk their welcome, Lady Blanche was brought into the hall. A very lily she seemed by reason of her grace, and Count Raoul spoke many fair words to her.

There was feasting that night at Sarzeau and those of Roche-Bernard drank deep, but the sons of Stephen held back from the cup. Then Count Raoul chid them for their carefulness, and John, Stephen's son, answered that there was a saying in the North that where wine entered, wit went forth. Count Raoul was angry at this and spoke in heat, but the men of Sarzeau held their peace.

Next day they rode out hunting, and Count Raoul was at the side of Lady Blanche. After a while, when the dogs gave tongue, he drew her aside from the rest into the forest, for he said to her that he hunted a lordlier quarry than the stag. Then, riding, my Lord spoke to her of love, as he so well could, saying among the rest: "Until yesterday, I laughed at love. I sought your father's daughter and kinship with him. But now the sweet pain I bear teaches me undreamed-of things—that your beauty, Lady, is more than name, a glance of your eyes worthier than all pride. Give me grace, then, that my life to the end may be full of your charity."

Lady Blanche said little to all this, for she was unskilled in words of the kind, but her eyes were glad. At last she answered softly: "Oh, dear my Lord, for all my love can be or do, it is yours indeed, and I will love you until I die."

Count Raoul hung his gold chain about her

neck for a token and kissed her lips. After a time, they rode back to the castle.

But when Lord Stephen saw the token and the face of his daughter, he strode forth alone in silence from the hall, and men said he had grown old overnight. As for Count Raoul, he laughed with his men at the ease of his wooing.

So Lady Blanche was married at Sarzeau, and Stephen Wolf bade guests from far and near; nor was there lack of meat and drink, or gifts for all who came, whether rich or poor. And glee-men were hired for dance and mirth. Seven days there was festival at the castle. Then Count Raoul made ready to ride back with his bride to Roche-Bernard, and Lord Stephen gave them rich gifts, one and all; but of his daughter he asked word apart.

When he had led her to his own chamber, Lady Blanche threw her arms about the neck of her father and wept long. Stephen drew her close to him and bowed his face. At last he said:

The Silver Girdle

"Do not weep, daughter. Do not weep. We of Eric's race never turn back from what must be, but meet it with steady eyes; and, having spoken, shrink not from the bargain."

She answered: "There is no thought of this, my father, but I weep at missing the sight of you and your strong love."

"That last," said Stephen, "you shall have always, here or elsewhere, if God wills. But there are some things I must say to you, and there is a gift to be given."

Then he went to his chest and drew forth a girdle of silver, cunningly wrought with figures of men and beasts. He placed it in her hands, and it was heavy to hold.

"Daughter," he said, "this is a token between you and me. I have watched Count Raoul of Roche-Bernard with these eyes which have seen many men, and I like him not—no, nor your brothers with me. Except for my word to his messenger, this wedlock should not have been."

Lady Blanche answered: "Father, I am now

Blanche of Roche-Bernard. I will not hear these words."

"Well spoken," said Stephen. "Cleave to your oath and your lord. But hearken. He has told you of love—this love of Maytime and kisses—that it endures. I tell you, no. It is wine soon poured. What then remains? In one case, nothing; in another, true deeds befitting comrades; in another, steadfastness and pride. These things are true. Now, touching that girdle in your hands. It was given long since to Eric the Viking by a Northern woman when they parted. And she laid a charm upon it that remains. Who clasps it on shall taste lonely sorrow and the pain of toil, but shall have strength to endure and the right of lordship. Take it then, but think well of the curse and the blessing if the time should come to wear it."

Lord Stephen raised his daughter up in his arms and kissed her, but he would not stay for longer speech. So they went back to the others. Yet, when they asked of my Lady what had been given her, she would not answer.

The Silver Girdle

Count Raoul and Lady Blanche rode forth from Sarzeau with their following, and her brothers bore them company for a time; but Stephen Wolf remained alone in the hall of the castle.

At Roche-Bernard the folk made ready a worthy welcome at the return of their master and mistress. Bonfires they made, and bells were tolled through the villages. Also, at night, there was drinking and dance in the outer court, while my Lord and his Lady looked on. But Count Raoul, being flushed with wine, seized in his arms a dark-haired girl, lithe and shapely, who was forward among the rest, and danced with her. Lady Blanche asked her name, and they said it was Nicollette, daughter of Antoine the miller. The castle of Roche-Bernard is but a grim place, lying apart from the road to Vannes, so there are few who come there, either fine company or those with new tidings. And for this reason Count Raoul was often away, guesting with friends or kindred, for he was bent on pleasure. Thus, Lady Blanche was overmuch alone for a bride, and the women who had followed her from Sarzeau talked among themselves, though she said nothing. Also, the rich broad lands that should have yielded full measure gave only a tithe, and there was want and idleness among the people. At this she wondered, since on the lands of her father men toiled from dawn to night, and the thriftless were whipped as a warning. Yet when she spoke of this to my Lord, he laughed and bade her look to her needle.

The year passed from summer to winter, and my Lady saw ever less of Count Raoul, but her great joy was in his return to the castle. Men said that she would watch hour-long from the tower, and hurry forth to meet him in the court. (At night also, she would hold his mantle on her knees when she was alone by the fire. But Jehanne, bowermaid, told others that once she had asked my Lady why she did not wear that goodly girdle of silver which was in her chest, and she began to weep, bidding the girl hide it away so that she might not see it.)

No fox can run too long but there is wind of him; and so it was with the doings of Count Raoul at Vannes and other places that the people in Roche-Bernard knew of them, and the girls in the spinning room tossed their heads and laughed. But they learned better, for on a time there came in to them Lady Blanche.

"I have heard there is chatter among you," she said, "touching the honor of your lord and mine, a gentleman—shameful words. Look to it, then, and keep your foolish tongues quiet between the teeth, or there will be the whip for each of you and bitter fare."

Scant red was in their cheeks when she left them. But that evening she stayed alone, and not even her woman could come in to her.

So also, by reason of Count Raoul's absence, gossip spread abroad the report that a gracious lady was much alone at Roche-Bernard.

But one day there came as guest my Lord's

cousin, a young man, Sir Christopher Saint-Pré, whom she received well as of kin. This one, when he had marked her kindness to him, grew bolder. At last he overreached himself, when they were in the hall. Then Lady Blanche rose from her chair, tall and white.

"*Beau sire,*" she said, "is there rust, do you think, upon the swords of Stephen Wolf and his sons? Answer me."

He said, "No," wondering.

"And is there rust upon their honor?"

"No," he said.

"Whose daughter think you I am, and of what race?"

He answered: "The daughter of Stephen, of the Barons of Sarzeau."

"You are a foolish man, *beau sire,* who can answer thus and know nothing more concerning me."

After this, she left the hall.

Next day, Count Raoul entered Roche-Bernard, and his cousin, who was a weak, sly man, complained of my Lady's harsh bearing to him, so that my Lord chid her for one who was ignorant of courtly manner. "Love words," said he, "are empty as the wind, meaning nothing." Then Lady Blanche could no longer shut from her mind the words of her father at their parting. Thereafter, it was said, she wept much in her loneliness, but she still watched for the coming of Count Raoul from his journeys and went to meet him gladly.

At last cruel winter, hateful to man and beast, was at end, and May returned to the land. There came also the day when a year had passed since the betrothal of Lady Blanche, and it chanced also that on this day Lord Raoul was in Roche-Bernard, but rode forth early into the nearby forest.

So, when he was gone, my Lady smiled, as with pleasant thoughts, and put on the gown she had worn at the hunting in Sarzeau. Around her neck was also the golden token he had given her, and she had her horse brought out into the court. She asked the gatesman which way my Lord had gone, and when he had told her, rode singing along that path. Thus she went through the forest, gay at heart with hope of their meeting.

A half league on, there was a woodsman at work near the path.

"Have you seen my Lord of Roche-Bernard?" she asked.

"Yes," answered the fellow, "for he rode by to his hunting lodge in the dell."

My Lady was all the happier at this, because it was a sweet, green place, deep in the woods. When she came near it, she leaped down from her horse and tethered him, stealing forward as a girl will to come unawares upon her sweetheart. So at last she drew to the clearing and looked between the trees down at the lodge. There she saw Count Raoul indeed, and he held Nicollette, the miller's daughter, in his arms.

Those who knew my Lady in afteryears, when

she rode with her men among the fields at sowing time and harvest, or when, seated in the hall, she passed judgment upon serf and freeman, will scarce believe that she once had the face of a girl, with tender eyes. For later she was firm in government, and there were none more able to hold their own; proud she was, and carried her head high. The line of her mouth was hard, and it was said she was most like Stephen the Wolf of Sarzeau.

Now, after she had stared down for a space at Count Raoul and that other by the lodge, she turned and walked blindly to her horse, and pressed her face against the saddle. Then she mounted and rode back along the path. The woodsman was still working with his ax. His name was François.

"Fellow," she said, reining up, "you told me truly that Count Raoul was in the dell, and here is pay for the tidings."

Whereat, she drew off the gold chain from her neck, that was her love-token, and tossed it to him. He clutched it in his hands and gazed after her.

In the court of the castle, she bade them bring out fresh horses for herself and her servants: "For I am minded to ride shortly for Sarzeau." Men wondered at her face, and Jehanne, bowermaid, knocked in vain at the door of her room.

Lady Blanche, when she was alone, walked back and forth; and at times she looked out over the fields of Roche-Bernard. But at last she went forward to her bridal chest and drew out the silver girdle of Eric. She raised it to her lips, kissing it, and with tears. Then carefully, paying heed to the clasps, she drew it on, heavy about her waist, and called in her woman.

"I shall not use today the horses for Sarzeau, but will send a message to my father."

And this is the letter she wrote to Lord Stephen:

That time has come, my father, for the wearing of the girdle which was a token between you and me. At first I yearned for you and my brothers, to seek com-

The Silver Girdle

fort in your arms. But it is borne in on me that those of our blood flinch not from their chosen path, be it good or ill. I have chosen and will bide the end with courage. Also the thought comes that we of good blood are bound as serfs to our place, in grief and joy. I will remember my vow to Raoul of Roche-Bernard, and will keep it with God's help, as befits a wife. I will strive for good to him and his folk. You also I will remember, and the pride of our honor.

From that day forward, Lady Blanche wore always the girdle of silver—and no other ornament, whether jewel or gold.

Nicollette

THIS story men tell of the dealings of Lady Blanche with Nicollette, daughter of Antoine the miller, when Count Raoul had ridden forth to the crusade. For there came words like flying sparks, strange rumor, and uncertain tidings. It was said that angels were abroad in Provence, great messengers, summoning to war. And there were visions, miracles, and dreams, tumult and gathering. But of all this the folk in Roche-Bernard could learn nothing for sure, and the days passed evenly. Until at last the very flame itself swept suddenly over it— that holy fire—and even this far-off Brittany was caught up in the heat of it.

Nicollette

It was on Midsummer that there rode up to the gates a band of cavaliers, well armed, with their followers, who wore, each man on his hauberk, a scarlet cross. And they cried: "Lower the bridge, you of Roche-Bernard, without fear. God's truce is in the land, and we bear His sign." When Count Raoul saw there were men of his kin among them, the gates were raised.

Who shall soon forget the wonder that night of how Urban, the Pope, at Clermont decreed war for the Cross? *"Deus vult,"* he had cried. And low men outrivaled their betters; nay, little children were even now on the march to Christ's city. And Godfrey of Bouillon and Lord Baldwin were leaving; Tancred the Norman, and Raymond of Provence, with others—so many that every bypath and highway through France was alive with horsemen. "And we ride to follow Lord Godfrey, who is the best of them. How now, Count Raoul," they challenged, "will you make one with us? No hurt shall come to your holdings when you go; for who dares anathema

and will break the truce? But for you is the blessing of God and assured salvation, honor in war
with good comrades. Strange lands we will see,
and rich. We shall guest with kings. Yes, and
there will be booty for the taking, fair and fine,
heathen plunder for the servants of Christ."

This was welcome speech to Lord Raoul, who
loved nothing so much as new things, pleasure
and change, so that he embraced that company
gaily and called for Michael, Mass priest, to bless
a cross for him. Meanwhile there was drinking
of wine and good fellowship.

But Lady Blanche, his wife, who sat apart
from the men and said little, asked of a sudden
whether the lords of Sarzeau, her father and
brothers, were making ready for this war.

"No," answered one, who was kin to Raoul,
"for Stephen the Wolf is old."

"But his sons, then—John and the rest?"

"They would have none of it," said the other
shortly, "answering that they would bide at
home, guarding their fields."

Nicollette

"Are they alone in this?" asked my Lady.

"Pardie, yes, except for like-minded fellows, careless of God and fame."

Count Raoul turned to her, and smiled a little.

"Are you of their sort?" said he. "Would you scant me of honor?"

"No," she answered. "Go forth and may you find it abroad, but take heed that you leave me as seneschal at Roche-Bernard."

It was said she craved the government of lands and castle, for she thought them poorly ruled, but a heavy burden it was for a woman.

The knights and their servants stayed on at Roche-Bernard until Count Raoul had taken the cross before the chapel altar and made ready his band for the march. Great cheer they had, both meat and drink. But at last all things were ordered. There followed my Lord's banner some fifty men, the best and strongest from the domain. When they were fitted with arms and horses, and Count Raoul had taken gold enough for his needs, scant were the hoardings in the coffers. Then, on a summer morning, they rode out, while men yearned after them and women wept. But my Lady turned back to the castle, after short farewells.

Yet this last memory Lady Blanche took with her: that there stood beneath the wayside cross a woman, who bore a child in her arms. She looked white and faint. Lord Raoul tossed her a gold piece, laughing. And the horsemen passed on, while those of Roche-Bernard pointed her out to their fellows as Nicollette, miller's daughter, who was paramour of my Lord. Then one who was last turned in his saddle and cursed her. He was Jacques, her brother, the son of Antoine. Only she neither saw nor heard him, for she was sunk down by the side of the cross, and her face was hidden in her hands.

Next day there came to the castle one Eustace, a cobbler, who, when his patching was done, sat down to meat and ale in the kitchen. When he had eaten a spell, "By God," said he, "I know a

maid with a sore back, if maid she can be called."
The others asked him his meaning. "Why, thus,"
he answered. "When I came by the mill this
morning, I heard thumping and curses and
screams in plenty. 'Peace be to this house,' said
I, knocking. When who should come out but
Nicollette of the mill, comely Nicollette that
was. But I should not have known it, friends,
by reason of her torn clothes and the blood on
her face and neck. Like a wild beast she was, that
made for the wood, screaming, but dragging a
child by the hand. Then came out her father
Antoine with a club, and crying: 'You drab
of lords, go to them for your victuals, and my
curse with you. They are proud, are they? So
am I.' "

The maids of the kitchen laughed much at
this, saying she had the right wage of her pride
and boldness, but the men pitied her and spoke
ill of Antoine the miller.

After two days in the forest—what because
of hunger and the needs of the child—Nicollette

crept forth to the castle and the gatesman looked aside when she entered.

"Give me bread," she begged, "for Christ's pity! And my child is well-nigh dead."

Then the wife of René, archer, who was a good woman, brought food to her.

Now, in those days which followed the riding forth of Count Raoul, Lady Blanche lost no time in making good her right as seneschal. And she named as her steward and land-reeve two servants of her father—Bertrand, who was called the Balafre, and Thomas, hard men, but skillful in management. For she said: "If my Lord rides to battle for the Holy Cross, he will need money and aid. We must work then, man and girl, at Roche-Bernard." So she went out to the fields, overseeing the harvest. There was no idling thereafter, or waste. Also in the castle she passed back and forth, keeping all to their task.

Thus it happened that she came upon Nicollette, with her child and the wife of René, in a small room which was apart and little used.

"What woman is this," said she, "who is so gaunt and hungry? Bruised she is, and torn! On my word, it shall go hard with those that have mishandled you. For none of my people shall starve, nor shall men use their women like cattle. I pity you from my soul. Who are you, then?"

The wife of René, archer, could not speak for fear, and the head of Nicollette was bowed. She sank down before my Lady and clasped her knees, saying: "Pity me, and give me only a corner where I may bring forth the child within me, and food that this other little one may eat. For the Virgin's sake, grant me mercy, and forgive!"

"What have I to forgive you?"

Then my Lady raised the face of Nicollette with her hand, and looking more closely, saw who she was.

The anger of Lady Blanche, Stephen's daughter, was not easy to bear. Strong men have shrunk from it. She spurned the woman from her and her eyes were grim.

The Token

"So!" she whispered. "Is it so, woman, that you weep here for mercy? Foul leavings of foul love! It shall go ill with you. I shall add blows to your bruises and rags to your rags. Mercy, quotha! And what right have you, drab and slave, to speak of children—*his* children—when *I* have prayed in vain, and longed. As for you," said my Lady to the wife of René, "get hence. You shall smart for this!" But when she had stood for a time looking at Nicollette, who cowered away from her and clutched the child, "Go!" she said, "before I think again of you and of my shame."

So the woman hurried forth from the castle, trembling and in tears.

There was an old wife who lived near the far field, in the woods—a basket maker. Her name was Alice and men called her witch, for wise she was truly in the lore of herbs, bitter of speech and ugly, being gnarled like a root. She sat by her door weaving baskets, and talked with those

who came for her counsel. Men said that fairies, whom the priests had banished, returned at night, teaching her ancient wisdom of the trees and stars. Therefore none went that way after sunset.

It was the custom of Lady Blanche, when days were hot, and she had overseen the fields, to draw rein by the well of Dame Alice and drink a cup of its water, which was clear and sweet. Then she would rest for a time in talk beneath the trees, or listen to olden stories of the gammer, and wise sayings. These times were very pleasant to her. But it was said that goodwife Alice set greater store by them than aught else, and kept my Lady's cup washed and clean, nor would suffer anyone else to touch it. And she hearkened eagerly for the sound of her horse.

So it came about on the noon of a day that my Lady rode thither, and was seated on a bench while the woman clipped rushes, when out from the hut there ran a young child, who hid her face upon the knees of Alice.

The Token

"How now!" said Lady Blanche. "Goodwife, you deal in wonders—and have you found this child, or is she kin to you?"

The other raised her eyes. "Men talk much of fairies hereabouts. What if this were a changeling of theirs? What think you of it?" My Lady crossed herself, but she wished well to the Good People. "Look at her," said the grandam. And my Lady, drawing her close, saw that the child was beautiful, with dark hair, but the eyes were blue and wide.

"This is no churl's daughter," she said; "the skin is white. How came she here?"

Dame Alice answered: "She came at night from the forest—a gift to me. Look again. Who so skilled in art could fashion the like—this hand or foot, this soft arm? What think you of my treasure?"

Lady Blanche took up the child. "If it were mine!" she said.

"Nay, there is more," said the old woman, "a rarer thing. Look in her eyes. They are clear.

They have no taint of evil-knowing that dims our eyes."

"It is the work of God," said my Lady, "the beauty of His thought. Oh, Dame Alice, tell me why came this gift to you rather than to me, who have yearned long years?"

Then Gammer Alice rose from her bench and said: "Will you have the child? And will you pay a price for her?" My Lady answered with joy that she would. "A great price?" She answered yes. "Then come," said the old woman, "come and pay!"

She went into the hut, and Lady Blanche followed her. In a corner was a bed of straw, and on it lay one who seemed asleep. When they came near, my Lady saw it was Nicollette, miller's daughter. She held a baby in her arms, and her eyes were open wide. Then, seeing my Lady, who looked down at her, she drew the child close.

"Why do you come?" she cried. "You shall not take him from me—my little son. Nor shall you drive me hence."

The Token

Lady Blanche turned, cold upon Dame Alice. "What is your meaning?"

"Find it in your heart," said the other, "and tell me whether you would rather hold hate in your heart or a child in your arms, for this is the price I spoke of."

The baby moved in the arms of his mother with a little cry, but she stilled him tenderly, laying bare her breast. And her eyes were filled with gentleness, yet fear, when she glanced up at Lord Raoul's wife. Lady Blanche spoke nothing, but she beheld upon the face of Nicollette a strange, noble beauty, which was born of pain with joy, and every taint of evil had been cleansed away. So it is that God works in this dark world.

Then, of a sudden, she cried out, half in grief, half lovingly: "Lo, I would rather be this woman on the straw, who has brought forth a child to love, than Lady of Roche-Bernard!" She leaned down and kissed Nicollette upon the forehead. "Have no fear of me, you mother! Honor be yours among men, as God honors you!"

Nicollette

Dame Alice drew her away. "It is enough," she said. "You have paid the price."

Not long after this Nicollette died, for the grief and hardness she had borne. And Lady Blanche claimed of Dame Alice the two children as her right. She rode thither with Bertrand Steward, who carried them before him to the castle. Goodwife Alice parted from them with tears, for she loved them dearly. The boy was called Pierre, and the girl Annette.

The Miracle

IT was not long after Count Raoul had ridden with my Lord Godfrey to the Holy War that there arose murmur and discontent among the serfs—Jacks, they were called—through the length and breadth of the demesne. And this was owing to a mad friar, Francis by name, whose words were like fleas in the ear. He came God knows whence, but he brought with him care in plenty, blazing ricks, and the death of men. Perhaps they set small store by the power of Lady Blanche, now that my Lord was gone; and had bided this time for rising, when a woman was seneschal in Roche-Bernard. But therein they missed their count, as you shall see.

The Miracle

By clearing and hamlet, sheepfold and cross-roads went Brother Francis, and his words were of this sort: "Behold, the time is at hand! Behold, Christ is the Saviour of churl and freeman, serf as well as lord. And upon me His hand rests, and the sound of His voice, crying: How long! Wherein, I am also glorified, though else of no account—Francis, the beggar, and yet messenger of One with whose voice I speak, saying: The harvest is ripe. The grapes of My wrath have I trodden out, and the red cup of My anger is full. Have My eyes not seen, with tears have they not seen your grief, O silent people, who dare not cry —yea, even unto Me ye dare not cry—whose face is turned to the dust? Have My hands not fingered your wounds when the whip was done? Have they held back from the scores of your collar? In the night, have My ears not heard the voice of your shame—the cry for those who will not return? Come! Have I not seen through the dark? Have I not smelled the flesh of your branding? And the forests I have planted for men bear the fruit of their bodies! But My anger is awake on the hills. It shall strike! Surely it shall strike! And My arm is bared for your salvation. For the time is at hand. Arise then; make free this land for the sunlight of your God, who rejoices in the joy of men, for He has made them. And truly I will bestead you in the battle, and ye shall prevail."

In this wise spoke Brother Francis; and wherever he passed rose fierce questioning and gathering of men, much idle speech and anger. For they took such blasphemy to heart and, brooding on it, were turned from reverence of their betters, until at last they banded themselves in mutiny.

This friar was a pale, slight man, and small of stature, but with strange power upon the people. Yet though his words were sharp and evil, his deeds were fair. Men said that he had the gift of miracle by the cures he wrought. And he was good to those in distress, seeking nothing for himself in return.

The words of the preacher fell upon no more

willing ears than those of Antoine the miller, who had a chief voice among his fellows. Though he was old, he had been of great strength and cheer until the shame of Nicollette, his daughter; but after Count Raoul's dealings with her, he wasted away, kept much to himself, nor worked with any will at his trade. It was thought he had not long to live. Now when the tidings of Brother Francis came to him, he went forth to find the friar and had him home to the mill. After that it was said that ten years had fallen from the shoulders of Antoine, and he busied himself much among the churls, far and near.

Thomas, land-reeve, had sent back cold reports of all this as he rode his circuit, bewailing the poor yield of the land and the sullen bearing toward himself—barefaced idleness of men and women. Nay, at St. Juste he had ordered the whipping of several as an example. Yet for all that, he sent back ever darker warnings to Lady Blanche, where she sat in the castle of Roche-Bernard; and in his smithy Simon, armorer, with his lads, was seen to be busy with war gear and weapons.

On a day, about the hour of Angelus, came a horseman wildly riding; and the gatesman, looking down, thought he was clothed in red, but glancing more closely saw it was a naked man and smeared with blood from head to foot.

"For God's sake," cried he from the horse. "Let me enter in haste, for I must have word with my Lady before I die."

Then they let him in. He was René, an archer of Thomas Land-reeve's. A cloak was thrown about him and he was carried before Lady Blanche, for he could no longer stand.

"Christ's pity!" she said, with a pale face. "What is this?"

"Messire Thomas is down," answered René, though he spoke heavily. "They have plucked the eyes from his head; his hands and feet they have struck off; and they have fixed him on a stake to die. His archers are all slain but me. When they had flayed me from waist to throat they let me go, that I might bear the tidings and their defiance; for they swore me to say to you, Lady, that where Roche-Bernard stands they would drive in the plow!"

He stretched forth his arms from beneath the cloak, and they were skinless tendons and dried blood.

"But who are those who have done this?" cried Lady Blanche in a cold voice.

"Who but the Jacks!" said René, laughing madly, for his wits were astray. "The Jacks, led on by Francis the priest—though he bade them have mercy. And they are burning the country-side as they go."

When my Lady heard these things, she rose from her chair and bent over René.

"You have a great heart, René," she said. "Be-hold, you shall have vengeance. And for your wife and children take no heed—they shall be first in Roche-Bernard."

The Token

She bade the castle folk tend him to the end as though he were Count Raoul himself.

The face of my Lady was grim to look upon when she turned away, and no one cared to meet her eyes. Yet she lost no words in anger—only bidding Simon Armorer look to the equipment of the men for war; and that very night she sent out a swift rider to Lord Hubert, her cousin, at Castle Neuf.

"What is your purpose, then?" asked Bertrand the steward.

He was an old man but skilled in arms, and had ridden with Stephen Broadaxe, my Lady's grandsire. There was a scar on his face. He was still called the Balafre.

She answered that she would ride to East Ford, and there meet with those from Castle Neuf. Together they would make head against the Jacks, and turn them off from Roche-Bernard with the outbuildings, which were rich from the harvest.

"But even thus," said Bertrand, "your force will be small; and if it fail there is scant hope for the castle. It were best to crave help from Vannes. You will muster a bare hundred as it is, but the serfs are twenty times as many."

"How long will it take for this help?"

"A week," answered Bertrand.

"But the barns," she said, "and our home fields?"

The Balafre shrugged his shoulders. "They would go to the flames, sure enough, but you save the castle."

Then the wrath that was in her leaped forth, and she struck Bertrand in the face with her hand. "Hearken," she said. "I purpose to guard these lands, as it is my duty. This, with God's help, I will do. Nor did I ever think to hear my grandsire's man whine for help, like a dog."

The Balafre stamped his foot for delight of her. "By God," he laughed, "you are a slight minx in your body, but with the heart of Broadaxe himself. A blessing I call it to have heard this."

So it was also that my Lady, armed, wearing

47

both hood, helmet, and camail, went with her men in spite of Bertrand's prayers. She bade them carry at her side the standard of Roche-Bernard. "Our Lady of Vannes," she prayed, "strike for our just cause!" They rode out, some forty in all, but left fear and grief behind them in the castle.

There was never a sharper fight in Brittany than fell at the village of Torchy. There the Jacks were gathered, and thither, when they had met, rode those of Castle Neuf and Roche-Bernard. With Lord Hubert came some famous gentlemen, who by good luck were his hunting guests —the holy Bishop Richard of Vannes, Sir John de la Tour and Sir Walter of Bruges, with their following, who were glad of this chance to show manhood.

In a field near the village was a knoll; upon it stood Brother Francis, unarmed save for a cross he carried, heartening the churls. "Strike now for your children," said he, "that they may live

as free men. Behold, your memory shall grow through the years, and beneath its shade shall they rest to bless your names. Great is the gift God gives you—there is none so great—to strike for His cause against evil. You shall prevail—lo, I speak with the voice of Christ—you shall speed well in this battle. Take heart! Fear nothing! Angels fight for you. And the night of your bondage shall pass before the dawning of your freedom."

He came down from the knoll, striding among the men to cheer them, and stood with his cross in the forefront of the battle.

The lords and their following now spurred in with high courage, although they were few against the line of the Jacks, and well did each man quit himself. But there was none had greater credit than my Lady Blanche, for around the banner of the Golden Leopard of Roche-Bernard the fight was always fiercest. It was said she struck down four men with her own hands that day. Bertrand Steward guarded one side of her, and Simon Armorer the other. Well also did Lord Hubert and the gentlemen with him do their part; so that, albeit the Jacks fought long and stubbornly, their ranks were broken at the last. They were many, but poorly armed with knives or scythes, and a great number had only clubs or stones. Besides which, it was soon plain that they could not deal with seasoned cavaliers.

This affair lasted three hours, and the dead among the serfs were piled high. Moreover, many were cut down as they fled, and many taken. Among these were Francis the priest and Antoine Miller.

"How now!" cried the miller to Francis the priest, spitting blood, for he was hard wounded. "Where are your angels and your victory?"

Brother Francis bade him take heart, for that God would not deny his servants but would save them surely by a miracle from heaven. Antoine laughed out at this and fell upon the ground, where he died.

At the bidding of Lady Blanche, all on her

side, with much jollity, rode back to Roche-Bernard, taking the wounded with them and the prisoners. These Lady Blanche had hanged that same day from the walls, as a warning to misdoers; and it was a matter for laughter that they all cursed Brother Francis for his lies, which had led them astray. He, because he was a priest, was left straitly bound beneath the castle.

That night a great banquet was held for the guests—my Lord Bishop, Lord Hubert, and the two good knights, Sir Walter and Sir John. There was much good cheer—both meat and red wine, laughter, and talk of the happenings of the day. All paid high praise to the courage of Lady Blanche. But, when they had eaten, she asked counsel as to what must be done with the friar, who was the root of this trouble. "He is only mad," she said, "and believes the truth of his words." The Bishop of Vannes struck the table with his fist, and said there were priests enough at board to deal with blasphemers. Richard of

The Token

Vannes was great of strength and stature, black of hair and beard. There were few but feared his anger. He called for a cup and drank it out. Then he said: "We will visit this friar; but bring wine with us, for the work may be hot." His priests and two men-at-arms followed him down into the dungeon.

After a space they returned, carrying with them Brother Francis, for his legs were broken from their handling of him and his eyes seemed as though starting from his head. They laid him on the floor near the chair of Lady Blanche.

"At last," said the bishop, "we have come to reason with the devil that haunts him, and have driven him forth. He blasphemes no more. Speak, you there, and say now whether you are the messenger of God."

For a time Brother Francis answered nothing; his face was whiter than flour. At last he spoke heavily. "If my flesh has denied Him, for the pain and the fear, my soul does not deny Him whose messenger I indeed am. And I have lived to His honor—yes, even in this hour."

When he had said this, he stretched out his arms and clasped the feet of Lady Blanche, as one who would ask pity if he dared, for great fear was on him.

The veins stood out upon the forehead of my Lord Bishop, and it seemed that he would have torn the friar with his own hands; but he cried out to his servants: "Back with him, then! Am I to be laughed at? For the devil within him shall squeak to another tune."

His men came forward to seize the friar where he lay trembling, but my Lady Blanche rose from her chair, and bade them stand off.

"There has been enough of this," she said; "it is not my will that you torment him further."

"But, by God," cried the bishop, "it is mine!"

Thus they stood facing each other. My Lady did not lower her eyes.

"Hearken, holy father," she said. "I rule in Roche-Bernard."

The other gentlemen and priests besought

Richard of Vannes to patience, for there should be no strife at a time of banqueting. And they brought him to his chair, filling a cup for him; but he vowed that the friar should burn next day.

"As to that," said my Lady, "I have no power."

She bade Bertrand Steward carry him with all gentleness back to the prison. And the guests sat long at their wine, but Lady Blanche went to her own chamber.

Now when all was still at last, in the dark hours before morning, Bertrand the Balafre felt a hand on his shoulder, and rising up saw it was my Lady that stood near him. "Carry this light," she said, "and follow me." Together they went down into the dungeon, while Bertrand wondered.

When they had come to the cell where Brother Francis lay, she bade the Balafre stand in the door, and herself went forward to the friar. He was awake, for it was bitter cold in that place, and his pains were great. He stared up at her and

she looked down at him, but neither spoke for a time.

At last she said: "How is it with you, Father?" He answered that it was well. "You are cold," she said, "and suffer, and are alone. Those who followed hate your name and curse it. Is this well?"

He answered: "It is the cup many have tasted before now—an honorable cup."

His voice was low, but very clear. It seemed to Bertrand Steward that it came not from the room but from elsewhere, a silent place.

"Who are you?" said my Lady. "I must ask you this here, alone. Whence are you? Like a fire you have passed, kindling the hearts of men— you so small and weak. Because of you there is death and sorrow. Is this of Christ, the bringer of peace?"

And the voice answered slow, far off: "As the marksman aims, so will the arrow fly. I was an archer's shaft."

Of a sudden, my Lady stretched out her hands.

"What of me, then? I have done no willful wrong. I have followed my path, for on me was laid my charge—to guard and rule. But if indeed you are His messenger, how great will be my doom!"

She stood with bowed head, gazing down upon the friar. She was clothed in white. Save for the torch, there was darkness around them. Then Bertrand the Balafre heard fair words, which he bore long in mind.

"Lady, God asks two things of men—courage and truth—no more. Why do you fear? Your soul is true and brave."

She cried out: "But if you are sent from Him, then I have wrought against Him. With my own hands in the battle I have defied my Lord."

Brother Francis turned his gaze full upon her. "Ask Richard of Vannes," he said, "and those with him who I am. But behold, I am in this place; my body is broken; my cause is lost; this day I shall die. How then? Have I not lied? Have

I not betrayed those who believed in me? Why should you doubt?"

There was silence when he had spoken, but the steward saw that Lady Blanche had knelt down, touching the knees of the friar with her hand.

"I pitied you in the hall," she whispered; "now pity me. I cannot understand these hidden things, who am but a child in the night. Only, my heart believes in you, even though you die today; only, I ask your blessing and your pardon, if this can be."

A sudden strange light came upon the face of Brother Francis. "Raise me," he said, "so that I may lean against the wall. I have something to say to you." When she had done this: "Lady, it is not strange we should meet, though late—you, daughter of lords, and Francis the beggar; ruler and rebel; for in Roche-Bernard tonight you alone are kin with me. It was fitting we should meet. Hearken then! I said that I was sent by Christ, and so I am. This you believe, and this is a blessing richer than I could give. I told of miracles from heaven. They have come to pass. Though in ignorance I dreamed of angel swords —lo, a greater wonder, beyond mortal dreams, that through pain and loss flows in a vision of the truth. So it has come to me here in the dark— my miracle of peace. And this much I will tell you of the mystery: You are as I am; neither needs the other's pardon."

His voice was low music, very sweet to hear. The Balafre strove hard to catch each word.

"Behold, in an organ there are many notes; only let each be true, and from them all the organist weaves out his harmony. Thus, upon a greater organ, God draws His music from various notes. Would sameness bring forth harmony? So is built the eternal anthem from various souls, finding its concord in the truth of each. King, churl, and priest—no matter. You have done your work, my daughter, and I mine—and yet not ours. May you have peace!"

My Lady had bowed her head upon the knees of the friar, and his hand rested long upon her hair. The Balafre turned away his face. At last, when she had risen, she asked if there were any gift for him within her power. He answered: "Yes; that I might be taken to look again upon the stars." So Lady Blanche bore the light, and Bertrand Steward carried Brother Francis up to the inner court.

That day, by order of the Lord Bishop, he was burned at the village of Torchy, where the battle had been. The churls were driven from far and near to witness it. So, in the fashion of their kind, they cursed him and cried out for miracles. Even when the flames were around him in his pain, they laughed the louder.

The Lay of the Oriflamme

MESSIRE Huon Le Roy had stayed the summer through at the castle of Roche-Bernard. That was a great delight and honor for all, you may believe; for in those days no master of song rivaled him, whether in the making of ballads or brave stories of ancient men. He was the hearth-friend of dukes and bishops through the length of France, so that his presence brought fame also to Roche-Bernard. Only it was a wonder that he should condescend to stay so long, when he might have had the best in the land, though nowhere more grateful love.

Even when the barns were full, he still rode

coursing with my Lady Blanche by day, and on
starry nights sang before all in the outer court.
He had tales enough for men and maids, and a
free laugh that was gay to hear.

At length there came frost to redden the leaves,
and cold north winds; whereat he sang no more,
but sat chin on hand with my Lady in the hall.
Then Isabeau, smith's daughter, who loved him
like the sun in heaven, wept, fearing he would
soon be gone. But Jehanne, bowermaid, rated her
soundly before the rest because she would set
herself up in grief, and told her plain there were
others to weep as well as she.

At last came a day when Messire Huon, looking skyward, saw the wild geese strain to the
south, so that he sighed, and attiring himself,
asked audience of my Lady for leave to travel.
"Friends," he said, with a laugh for the comfort
of his hosts, "geese and singers are birds of a
feather. Whither one flies, there flies the other."

He was no ragged stroller. He wore a gold
chain around his neck, broad and fine, and he

wore a scarlet cloak with a cap to match, edged in ermine, and there was a peacock's feather held by a brooch at the side. But with all that, he had a long sword at his thigh with a hilt of gold, large in the grip, for he was skilled in arms. So, cap in hand, he sought out my Lady where she walked in her garden.

There were those who held Lady Blanche to be proud and cold. Certain it was that she kept both girls and men to their work, nor suffered any slackness in the management of households or lands. Moreover, she kept her own counsel and was short of speech. But she was the chatelaine of Roche-Bernard, and upon her fell the weight of government. Slight she was and fair, but with a lily's grace. She was ever plainly dressed, save that she wore a girdle of silver. Whether for piety or stainless name, through all Brittany there was none more highly praised. She delighted in Messire Huon's songs, and rode gladly with him to the forest.

Now when Messire Huon stood before her in

the garden, she gave a little cry, seeing him dressed to depart.

"My Lady," he said kneeling, "I crave a last gift of your favor, namely, that I may ride hence. Summer is past, and we singers are pursuivants of the sun. Look up and you will see the lines of wild birds, which beckon south."

Lady Blanche answered nothing to this, but asked that he walk a space with her in the garden. It was a pleasant ground, though small and narrowed in by the eastern walls. In season there were roses there, and there was an oak tree in the midst for shade, but its leaves were then falling.

When they had walked for a time, my Lady said: "We had hoped for you through the winter, when days are short and there is little cheer. Your songs bring Maytime thoughts. But I know well that we could not expect so far. Richer gifts are to be had elsewhere, and you have long delayed."

Then Messire Huon vowed that he sought no rewards. "For," said he, "when I rode hither and saw your walls, I half turned, thinking this but a grim place and poor; yet being come, when I saw my Lady in the hall, I thought: 'Here is a pearl set in an iron ring.' Therefore, I looked and saw you fair, but sad with the face of St. Agnes in Rouen church, so that I strove by the craft of song and rhyme to bring light to your eyes and a smile. There could be no higher wage."

My Lady Blanche answered: "If you seek no reward but the joy you bring, stay with us then; for well you know that in the princely halls of kings and holy bishops there is much delight, but here none. They have all pleasant things— music each day, and new sweet songs, but here, when you are gone, there will be no songs again."

After this she was silent awhile as they walked to and fro.

"Yet I know well, Messire Huon, what it is you lack with us—you, who have passed from court to court and know all that is wise and good, beautiful and famed."

But he shook his head.

"Therefore," said my Lady, "I have only a

thankful heart that this distant, small place should so long have harbored Huon Le Roy. Nay, I bid you good-speed, and Bertrand, steward, has certain gifts from me to you for a grateful token—though I could wish them richer and greater."

Then the good minstrel thanked her in fitting words for her favor to him, and vowed that *The Lay of Blanche the Chatelaine,* in praise of her, should be known wherever in France he sang before worthy men. Thus they walked to and fro in the garden, and Messire Huon was in no haste to take his leave.

She asked him whither he rode—to what castle or abbey. And he answered it was to none of these.

"Then," said she gently, "it is plain you seek the love of some young maid. Tell me of her."

Messire Huon laughed, but fell silent and sought long for words.

"You speak truly," he said. "It is love indeed I seek, but with shame."

The Token

She asked: "How can that be, my friend?"

And he answered: "It is with shame a pilgrim turns from his shrine. Noble lady, I have been here like one who breathes mountain air, yet returns weakly at last to the plain. Such is the love I mean, and of this you, highborn, can know nothing."

"Tell me of it, then," she said.

"I will tell you this much," he answered. "There is a white road in Provence, leading south through vineyards to the sea. Thronged it is with weary men and beasts. Until at last, through the dust, you reach a tavern set apart beneath cool trees. There are vine-green arbors here, a courtyard well of fair water—the freshness of Paradise to those worn by the hardship of that blazing road. And there in the shade stands a girl of the South, lithe and strong, black-haired and brown of skin, that cries welcome to all. The light of her eyes is like the play of dark water above gold.

" 'Enter,' she cries. 'Here are melons, cooled in the brook; here are purple figs, ripe and bursting! Would you have wine—new wine, sharp to the taste, and sweet? Would you have old, drawn from the cave? Then come! New wine for new love, I say, old wine for memories! Here are cheeses, fat as a friar; nut bread to suit; spice from Marseilles; baskets of grapes heaping over. So come then! Will you have kisses and dance? Here are girls from the land, fresh and free. Come then! A red moon tonight, but the shadows fall deep. You there, come in! Drink and love free of care—what is better? Free of *shall-nots* and *should-nots*—what's better? Come, buy of my wares. Ye are fools else. For why? Let me tell you, my masters: Death at your elbow whispers, *Live! I come!'*

"Thus," said Messire Huon, "the girl sings. I shall not ride by, for she tells the truth—at least to us singer-folk. And in that hostelry I shall seek to forget."

"What?" asked Lady Blanche very softly.

"You," answered Messire Huon, but he dared not look up at her face.

73

The Token

Then my Lady put her hand upon his shoulder. He felt that it trembled.

"Why should you forget me, friend?"

"Because I turn from your shrine. Nay, if I were only a little worthy, here I should stay to worship. I, who sing of noble love, have found it here—great because hopeless; fine since there's no attaining but knowing that through adoration comes peace at last. Yet I am one of the accursed who know in vain, who see heaven and cling to earth, who must be free for their own ruin, and go in motley all their days. I am a child of the carnival—singer as I am—and with the love of its roses at my heart. Yet I am ashamed, knowing your soul and high honor, that I stand so far below."

My Lady leaned against the tree where the leaves were falling. For a time she answered nothing, but gazed out at the sky above the walls.

"Nay, good Messire Huon," she said at last, "I thank you for all these things. But what if this saint you speak of wearied of her shrine and

74

vigil; craved love, not adoration; stepped down from her altar, out to the sun and you—what then? Would you despise the saint?"

He looked at her quickly and saw the brightness of her eyes. She leaned toward him with parted lips.

"You speak high words," she said. "Is it of courtesy only? Have they fire within? Tell me, would you despise the saint?"

His face answered her.

"Would I might go with you!" she cried. "Have I alone no right to life, who am sick of schooling, weary of duty, even this honor you speak of! Could I not laugh and love, crowning myself with roses! Do you think me cold—remote? Nay, kiss me and take me hence, before you as you ride, away to that green hostelry, a minstrel's woman. So you give me love, what care I! What care I, fulfilling the never answered longings! Would you pour me wine between the kisses? Would we dance in the moonlight, love in the shadows, unreproved? Then on, in the merry jostle of the world, from place to place and land to land! You shall teach me your songs, to sing them, your squire, pardie, in court and market place. Have I said enough? Have I made it plain that I am no saint?"

The heart of Messire Huon leaped within him as she spoke, for she was very beautiful and tender, with a strange light in her eyes, and her head leaned close to his breast. Then he caught her in his strong arms and kissed her hair and face.

"By heaven," he said, "I will hold you against the world! Love you shall have indeed, and song in your honor, wilder, sweeter than Tristram's of Iseult, until in other days men shall tell with bated breath of your beauty. Do you stoop to Huon the Singer? But he will crown you with love and fame. At Life's banquet, whether brief or long, we shall drink of the same rich cup, and Death shall not strike us asunder!"

"But the saint you worshiped, *beau sire?*"

"My Lady, I dreamed a foolish dream, and wake to find that earth is heaven."

The Lay of the Oriflamme

So they spoke for a time as he held her close, beside the trunk of the oak tree which shut them from the castle. He told her much of the road they would ride—the goodly cities and rivers—and her eyes were ever on his face, until, when he pointed to the south, she looked up and saw my Lord's banner streaming from the eastern turret. Whereat she hid her face against him. Then in fair words he painted the rich French lands—Touraine, many-castled, the smooth-flowing Loire—but when she raised her eyes, it was to see again the banner of my Lord, straining in the wind. At last she spoke.

"*Beau sire,* look and tell me what you see there on the eastern turret?"

He answered: "Only Count Raoul's standard tugging at the staff, for the wind is keen."

And she asked: "Will he be loosed, think you, or carried away?"

Huon wondered at the question, but answered no, for that the binding cords were strong.

"But suppose," she said, "that the cords were

loosed, would he not be borne high for a time, on the swift wind between earth and heaven, far over woodland and meadow from these walls?"

"If the wind held, he would."

"But at last, soon or late, sink to the earth, to become at the end a rag stained with dust, his blazonings gone—a beggar's clout, perhaps?"

"Nay, it might happen so."

"But now, bound to his irksome staff, and longing out upon the wind, he is a banner still, the Golden Leopard, hailed from far. Look again, Messire Huon. Do you see nothing else on the turret?"

"No," he said.

"Your eyes are dim, my friend. I am that oriflamme."

Then Lady Blanche bowed her face upon her hands. But afterwards, drawing apart and from him, she stood as if alone, gazing far off.

"That staff will never yield, beloved! Truly the days will come when, frayed and thin, the banner shall have served his use. So it is with women who are set aloft, apart, bound by stern laws. But if we descend, what then?—And yet, my singer, let this at least avail me, that henceforth, in court or bower, when others seek your love, you may recall my yearning and this pride."

Huon Le Roy knelt before Lady Blanche, laying both her hands upon his head in token of fealty, and she gave him a token for remembrance that her love would follow him until the end. Then he bade farewell, though shortly, for the pain at his heart. Men saw that his face was white when he mounted in the outer court. And it was many years before he was seen again at the castle of Roche-Bernard.

But in her honor he made *The Lay of the Oriflamme*. So it was known what passed between them in the garden.

The Conversion of
Abbot Gervais

IT is well known that once in this land there was neither church nor cross, font nor chalice. Then the fairies ruled—they who make paths of the moonlight and steeds of the wind. They were wise and merry, for they knew that a rose must die but danced the more blithely among its fallen petals knowing also that others, and fairer, would be. They brought love to men, for a jest or hate as it pleased them—good luck or ill, it was the same. Little children they lured to fairyland. And young girls pined in vain for gracious lovers seen only in the passing of the moon. They would not outstay the dark, these cruel ones, but their kisses were sweeter than

sweet wine. Fine music the fairies had—so rare
that those who heard their flutes, whether by sea
cliff or coppice, forgot the needs of life—the care
of fields and cattle whereby we live, but they
forgot never that melody, hearing it always, and
spent their years in wayward dreams. Yet
whether they were good or ill, men loved the
prankish folk, and on holidays set out for them
cakes and morsels. They lighted candles for them
also in the forest or by the hillside.

But when God's word had come to Brittany,
the shadow of the Cross fell dark upon the
fairies, and their charms were broken. Holy
priests from the South taught Christ in the land,
with urgent warning that these spirits were not
of Him, but rather of Satan, our enemy. "Wherefore, be rid of demons," said they. "Would you
worship devils with sacrifice and candles? You
pitiable men! Nay, cast them out with prayer.
Hear heaven's music, and flee that of hell. Be also
without fear, for what shall harm him who is
signed in God's name?"

The Token

Thereafter, the flutes of the fairies were heard less and less, and they could not abide the tolling of the bell. Nor were they often seen, but hid deep in the forest or crept out fearful on certain nights. Less and less were candles lighted for them —only by stealth, because heavy was the penance laid on him who forgot the new word for the old deceit. And little children were no more lured to fairyland, nor girls entranced by elfin sweethearts.

In this good work of salvation, none there was more steadfast than Gervais, the abbot. He was a plain, true man, toiling for the good of his lands like the rest, but took heed, as became him, to the cure of souls. Therefore he was well beloved. Only in one purpose he abated nothing, but was hard and grim: to wit, that he would uproot and utterly drive out what worship of demons still lingered on the countryside. "For it is shameful," he said, "and foul, that when the very stall-cattle kneel on Christmas night in Christ's honor, you should find willful men who light candles in the devil's honor. This shall not be!" And he set his hand to it so heavily, what with floggings and forfeits, that there were no more fairy tapers kindled in a course of years. It was said the elf-folk grieved at this, being cast out from the hearts of men.

At this time, two children ate at the high table of Roche-Bernard with Lady Blanche, the chatelaine. They were baseborn, although of noble blood, for their father was Count Raoul, lord of the domain, but their mother was Nicollette, a peasant's daughter. When Count Raoul had gone to the crusade, my Lady, his wife, who was childless, cared for them as her own, for loneliness of heart. Of these, one was Pierre the Cripple, lame from birth. The other was a girl, Annette. Men called her the Lark of Roche-Bernard. She had a voice of silver, and was light of foot, debonair and gay. Comely she was, with the dark hair of her mother, and fine blue eyes.

In those days she was ten winters old, so that she could ride out on a small horse with my Lady, and was cherished by all. But of the common folk, none loved her so well as Grandam Alice, the witch, who lived in a hut near the far field. The child came gladly to see her when she had leave from the castle, for Dame Alice was skilled in tart-making of wild berries, and she knew old, strange stories and rhymes. They two were faithful friends. Through the land, no woodsman there was but had seen them together, seeking strange flowers and hidden herbs. Surely also the child learned from her gammer more than horn-books knew, of forest ways, the wisdom of bird and beast, the uses of root or blossom for man's good or bane. But most, she learned tales of the forgotten times—of mighty men, proud women, anger and doom, the thunder of old gods; tales also of the elfin folk who had ruled our land. These she loved best. And witch Alice said: "There was no harm in their music, which I heard when I was young, though the music of Christ be deep and strong, for who would liken the song of a bird to the surging of the tide?

But their music gave rainbow colors to the life of men, which is dark enough." Then she told how the fairies fled. "Your foster father Gervais, the abbot, deems them an evil race. What should poor Alice know?—for he is wise. Only you may hear them mourn upon the wind at night."

Annette hearkened to these things with wide eyes. And she loved to dance upon the green elfin rings in forest clearings.

"There is danger in that," said Alice.

" 'Tis in their honor," said Annette. "Wherefore then should they harm me with mischief or spell?"

Once, too, with none but the grandam there, while they sat by a brook, she lighted a small taper. "Have joy thereof, banished folk," she cried, "for here is one that remembers you." Also it was her fancy to hold herself an elf-maid, playing quaint games alone and singing rhymes. It was pleasant to look at her, and hear. Annette brooded much upon the sad estate of the fairies. She said of the angels: "I will not love them, for they are fat with praise." And she said to my Lady, her foster mother: "I shall go to fairyland and comfort the elves, who are kin to me."

Lady Blanche answered: "Go then to that country if you can, and glad would I be, Annette, if I might find that path again."

"You knew it once, *ma dame?*"

"Yes," said my Lady. "Once."

Thus it came about on a May morning that Annette stole out to the forest when none was aware. And they sought her vainly in Roche-Bernard; nor had Dame Alice seen her. Two days they searched, but could find no trace.

Abbot Gervais was now an old man, bent with the years. More and more he had let slip the burden from his shoulders upon stronger ones, such as Brother Paul, the almoner; and it was his custom often in fine weather to walk out along the woodland paths, choosing silent ways which he called his cloisters. So on a day in early summer he had gone forth, and because the sun was high and his robe heavy, he seated himself beneath an oak—later named for him—a great tree of many branches. There he hearkened to the song of the sweet birds and a light wind in the leaves. He made a pillow of his cowl and watched the sunrays wink and pass. Then he fell asleep.

It was a gentle touch that wakened him, for looking up, he saw a young child sitting within his outflung arm. But at the moment he did not know her, seeing only dark hair crowned with violets, and wide blue eyes.

"What are you, little fair thing?" said Abbot Gervais.

"I am an elf-maid, Father," answered the other.

The good abbot sat up and crossed himself. "God forbid," he said; but looking again: "I know you now, pretty truant, for all my dim eyes. No elf or demon so comely as you are, foster child, in this land. And you are Annette of Roche-Bernard."

"It may be," said the girl, "but I am a fairy for all that, by the word of my Gammer Alice, who is a witch."

The Token

The abbot laughed in his beard, and raised her chin with a finger. "Well, be it so, elf-maid. And what would you have with poor Gervais, alone in the forest?"

Little Annette drew his hand down upon her knees. "Behold, Father," she said, "I do not come here of my own will, but am sent by the fairies to you, their enemy."

"Speak then, sweet messenger," he answered.

"I am to ask you questions without fail—grave questions, for the elf-folk know you to be wise and learned. First, then, dear Father: Who made the fairies?"

Abbot Gervais looked into her eyes, which were deep and true, and bethought him not to smile. "Truly God made them," said he; "for is He not Creator of all things, whether above the earth or under it, as He tells us plainly in His book?"

"Then, my Father, did He make them evil?"

"I tell you no," said the abbot, "for He is wholly good; but they, being left free, fell to

their own devices and loved the work more than its Maker, wherefore they clave to the earth and sea, forgetful that these are temporal; but being spirits, there remained to them beauty and power in measure; and being evil, they used this for the deception of man and his eternal loss."

"How do you know these things, my Father?"

"Wise men have written them, inspired of heaven."

"And that is why you do not love the fairies?"

"It is so," answered Abbot Gervais. "They are foes to God."

The child was silent for a time, and sad. "Poor little ones!" she whispered. "But tell me, Father mine, would you love them if they turned from ill and were christened—truly going to Mass, with other pious works? Say now."

The abbot puffed out his cheeks, but seeing her earnestness, strove with himself. "Girl, girl," he said, "that could not be, for surely they are damned spirits, and for such there is no turning."

"Did the wise men write it so?"

"Nay, but it is true, foster daughter."

"Yet, my Father, if it were not true, would you love them then?"

My Lord Abbot drew her close and kissed her. "Aye, then, if it were not true, I would love them."

Annette rose up, and dropped upon one knee as befitted a messenger. "Hear, then, O Gervais, Abbot of St. Rémy, the suit of the elfin folk, the boon they ask of you: that once only in the year, at Midsummer's Eve, their candles may be lighted by hillside and spring, to be a token of men's love, should they amend their ways. And truly, Father in Christ, I think we should not withhold our pity, but give it freely to all who ask for it."

Abbot Gervais frowned and answered: "Foolish child, what can you know of these things?"

But Annette put her face down upon his hand and held it so. Then, as he sat twisting his beard, there came strange thoughts to him of forgotten words that dealt with the minds of little children and a heavenly kingdom, and he muttered to himself: "Who am I that would gainsay it?" There came also memories of past years—their blossom and the faith, like hers, Annette's. Remembrance of death he had, the pity needful for him, Gervais, to cleanse out the toil-stains of his pilgrimage. Thus he sat with bowed head. And at last he spoke:

"Be it as you will, dear foster child. Shall a beggar deny bread to beggars? Let the candles burn Midsummer's Eve in token of our love, that be they elves or demons, they may know God's love through us."

So it was the next Midsummer, while folk danced and made sport, you saw near and far the shining of tapers. It was said also that there was music of flutes heard on the wind. This custom has remained. Men loved Annette the more for it, and they are called Annette's tapers to this day. But whether the fairies, so entreated, were brought from mischief to repentance was never learned.

From Him
That Hath Not

WHEN Stephen of Sarzeau came to
die, he sent the knife he had worn
to Lady Blanche, his daughter,
with these words: "Here is a blade which men
have called *Fang of the Wolf*. Link it, I pray you,
to the silver girdle I gave you once, for they two
belong together."

These were the days when there passed up the
highway, one by one, bands of men returning
from the East. And there were some who sang
holy anthems, and others evil rhymes; but many
rode silently, looking only at the path.

My Lord Raoul had sent back few tidings in
all the years since he parted from Roche-Bernard

From Him That Hath Not

—only demands for gold and men. Once, also, a ransom had been paid for him when he was taken prisoner, which had stripped Roche-Bernard bare. But others said that he had borne himself bravely at Acre and Tripoli; yet it was rumored that he was reckless in love and dice, and was best known for that among the followers of Baldwin.

Lady Blanche knew nothing of this last, for it was kept from her. It was her joy to picture out his glory, the sure honor he had gained, and she took pride in it for the sake of Roche-Bernard. "Indeed," she said once to a certain gentleman, "Lord Raoul was a boy at heart before this war, with a boy's heedlessness, but now, wearing the cross and in God's battle, his soul is strengthened. I know there will be good years for him and for me when he returns. He will take no second place among his peers in this land. And this shall be my crown." Therefore, as the winters passed, she toiled for the domain, making it yield more and more, and was proud to supply his needs, large though they were, and gave unstintingly. For she said, "It is in the cause of Christ and honor. Let us do our small part, since he bears the greater burden."

Now when she knew that the horsemen who rode by on the main road were of Lord Baldwin's part—he who ruled in Jerusalem—she posted messengers along the highway to ask news of her husband. But the crusaders only laughed when they spoke. So these men passed day after day, until none others came.

Then my Lady said: "This also is ground for pride to us, for because of his great heart he will not hasten to leave the work of God, but rather strives on among the last."

She looked no more for him, and recalled those she had posted on the road. Thereafter a fortnight went by.

It happened on a day at twilight that the gatesman saw a band of men ride out from the forest. There was overcast, rainy weather so that he

could not read their blazonings. They drew near,
within his hail asking who they were. "Fool,"
answered one who rode ahead, "are you blind?
I am Raoul of Roche-Bernard." Then he saw the
arms of my Lord on his shield, and shouted back
these tidings into the castle while he worked the
windlass of the bridge.

There was running and calling below stairs
and above. Young and old came out into the
court while the gate was raised. And some looked
for fathers or husbands, some for brothers or
sons among that troop which should ride in.
Women peered through the dark with wide eyes.
My Lady Blanche stood at the foot of the stairs;
her hands were clasped before her.

But there were heavy hearts that night within
the walls, for of those who had gone forth with
Count Raoul or had followed later, here was
barely a score. And whereas at their parting,
none were better mounted or braver armed, it
was a gaunt and beggarly company, this—
clouted and torn, a part on broken horses and

some afoot. For a space, you heard only some cry or greeting; but then the ranks were overborne by those of the castle, with embracing, laughter and babble on the one side, while many were they who questioned eagerly, and afterward stood apart in tears or silent.

Count Raoul sat for a time in his saddle, and looked about him. Then my Lady came forward to his stirrup. And there was one who carried a torch, so that she saw his beard was white upon shrunken cheeks.

"Raoul, my Lord," she said.

"If it pleases you," he answered. He swung heavily from his horse, and, the light falling on her: "Lady, I did not know you for the dark. Give the light here!" Then he took the torch and held it close. "I left you pretty, with fair hair and skin. You are wrinkled now." She answered yes. Count Raoul reached back the torch, and went with my Lady up into the hall.

Whatever of good there was in meat and drink

was brought forth that night to feast those who had returned. On the kitchen hearths great fires roared, with laden spits before them, and kegs of ale were rolled in from the buttery. In the hall there was steam of roasted flesh, good warmth from the flames, a storm of voices. Then, at the lower board, when they had eaten, brave were the stories of those foreign countries—how they had feasted and starved, of the sack of cities, of heathen women with elfin eyes. And they told of skirmish and battle, pagan giants and enchantment. "By the Virgin," said Jehanne, who was bowermaid to my Lady, "there are, sure, no men as brave as you."

But when the drinking was at its merriest, and everyone was agape for wonder, Eustace the cobbler spoke up and said: "These are proud things you have done and seen, but in all your telling, no word has been of holy miracles or grace from God to you who fought for Christ's city. What saintly deeds or visions were there? We would hear gladly."

The Token

One answered: "There was the Holy Lance of Antioch." But the rest were silent, until at last Gaultier, an archer, broke out laughing, and emptied his cup. "Hear now, good Eustace," said he, "and keep it between your two ears. In the outset, there was much talk of crosses and prayers, and of setting free that Holy City, for thus it is you get men to hazard life and limb. But we soon had the itch for land; it was clear that there were other quarries in the war than salvation. Besides, Eustace, we were plain men with bellies. Therefore, be sure that what you speak of was mockery to all but fools. May we have grace from heaven, I say, after dinner." Gaultier hugged a girl to him, and all laughed at the cobbler.

At the upper table, Count Raoul dined with my Lady but had few words for her. Yet when she prayed him to tell her of honorable deeds there in the Holy Land, he spoke somewhat of himself, and the renown he had, but little of others.

From Him That Hath Not

"Dear Lord," she said, "I thank God that you have won this fame in His cause. And now you shall rest, for you have endured great hardship."

He answered: "Yes, I shall rest, as you say."

There was sickness upon him, seeing that his hand trembled, and his voice was thick.

Then my Lady asked how it was that he returned so poorly equipped both in horses and arms, and he fell into anger. "It is because of you," he said, "who might have sent gold in plenty, yet would rather fatten your coffers while I lived poor."

She cried out it was not true. Count Raoul filled his cup and smiled.

So they sat before the fire while he drank; and there was grief about the heart of Lady Blanche, who saw that he was the same—only those years had taken from him the strength and beauty which she had loved. But she thought: It is maybe the sickness, and I am hard in judging. She sent forth and had brought in his two children, Pierre and Annette, placing them before him.

"Who are these?" he said.

"They are yours by the miller's daughter, and I have brought them up to be a joy to you."

"Thanks for your charity," said Count Raoul, "but where is their mother, who was a comely girl? Bring her to me."

Lady Blanche answered coldly: "Nicollette died long since."

My Lord turned from the children. After a time, he said: "How shall I know them to be mine, then? You are hot enough beneath your ice, *ma dame*. And was there not talk in our camp of Huon the *trouvère,* who made songs for you, and was guest overlong in Roche-Bernard?"

Now, my Lady sat close to Count Raoul, and he that served them saw her face was like stone; and of a sudden he saw that the knife she wore, Stephen the Wolf's, was at my Lord's throat, so that the point pricked in. Count Raoul's eyes fell

from her gaze, and she put the knife back in its sheath.

A long time no word was spoken. Then he said: "Lady, I know well you have kept your state and your honor. Have good of them! Maybe I have spent mine. What of that? Who cares when we have crawled into the earth at last?" He stretched out the wine cup, and it shook within his grasp so that the wine splashed down. He laughed and pointed. "Behold, you have not long to wait, highborn chastity. I am of those who can say: We have lived."

Thenceforward, Count Raoul was three years a-dying, by reason of the sickness which he carried with him from Palestine.

Pierre the Outcast

TOWARD the bitter end of his life, Count Raoul of Roche-Bernard was a man of strange humors. It was his custom in Lent to keep little Pierre the Cripple, his son by Nicollette, miller's daughter, always at his side, but at other seasons he would not endure the sight of him if it could be helped. Little Pierre had a back twisted from birth, so that he was ill-grown and white of face, though with fine eyes. Men said that it was sharp penance for my Lord, who was high and proud, to keep before him the last of his race, misbegotten, and crippled at that. But so it was; and through the whole of Lent, Count Raoul dealt kindly with little Pierre.

Pierre the Outcast

Thus was my Lord's penance high feast time for the child, who longed for Lent when others rejoiced at Christmas; and he used to say, when his pain was on him, that he feared he should not live till the next Ash Wednesday. Indeed, he might well fear it, for his weakness grew apace, and he could no longer walk with the small crutch he had but must be carried here and there. Little Pierre was well loved in the castle by men and girls, for he suffered much with closed lips. Nay, he was on the rack during life, but bore it patiently.

And yet there was one thing which was a very grief to him, whereof he spoke at times. For he would have been a knight—forsooth with his twisted body—to have taken the cross, like his father, and ridden among brave men, silly child that he was. Men said that he did not understand my Lord's bearing toward him, for God is merciful. But when Ash Wednesday came, it was as though the light of heaven shone upon his face as he sat before Count Raoul's knees in the great hall. Then he would pour forth questions he had hoarded through the year, touching noble men and deeds of arms in Palestine, the blessed field of Acre, and the stout French chivalry. Count Raoul answered him in full, though he was prone to speak overmuch of his own valor, the wounds he had suffered, and hardships undergone. Little Pierre would sigh for very happiness, and fall asleep at length with a question on his lips.

It came about at last, when the penitential season was at hand, that he was carried from his bed, wrapped in warm skins, and placed at my Lord's feet before the fire. Lady Blanche sought to turn him from this, for she loved him well and he had been much in pain during the day, but he pled so hard, and with tears, to hear my Lord speak that she could not bear to deny him.

So he lay before the fire breathing sharp, with pale lips, but his eyes were fixed on Count Raoul's face. Then my Lord told of the onslaught at Antioch, the forest of spears with gay pennons like birds aloft, the glitter of arms and the crimson shields, the war cry of famous chevaliers. He told him how he had wrought nobly that day amid the crash of the axes until his leg was broken by a stone slung from the walls. "By God," said my Lord, "that was pain a man would not lightly endure." So, in spite of his courage, he had been robbed of the rich prize he had hoped in the taking of the city. And little Pierre the Cripple looked up at him with shining eyes.

When his father had done, he breathed deep once or twice, and then, because the fever had unsettled him, asked in his shrill voice whether he might hope ever to be made knight. But when Lord Raoul heard this question, the lines of his mouth set hard and his anger and grief boiled over.

"Little toad," said my Lord, "is it not enough for my sins that I must see before me the broken end of a brave line, but I must also be mocked by you!" And he arose and kicked the child fiercely where he lay, crying out with grim laughter: "A knight!"

Lady Blanche called shame upon him, but he thrust her aside in his fury and left the room. Then she raised up little Pierre in her arms, but his eyes were closed. And she carried him with tears up to her own bed, and bathed his face, speaking soft words between her sobs, for the boy had been much with her. But his eyes were still closed and breath was hard.

Then came Don Michael, the chaplain, who was skilled in sickness, and said Pierre the Cripple would scarce outlast the night. He gave him holy unction and spoke the sacred words. Lady Blanche looked on with a white, cold face. Then came my Lord, Count Raoul, downcast and ashamed, who asked soberly what was amiss.

"You have killed him," said Lady Blanche.

Count Raoul drew a chair to the bed, and sat staring into the darkness beyond. So he stayed, not moving through the night, but it was said his face was fearsome to behold.

Pierre the Outcast

Now it befell that, as Count Raoul looked into the darkness, he was suddenly aware that he saw before him no longer darkness, but a swift, black river, where was a ford, and in the middle of the ford sat one in armor on a white horse. On the hither side of the river was an old woman, who washed a long white cloth. Then there came down to the bank, upon this side, little Pierre the Cripple, alone and leaning hard upon his crutch.

"You cannot cross here, little toad," said the one in armor with a laugh, "for this is the path of brave knights and gallant gentlemen. And who are you, with your withered legs and your crutch?"

Little Pierre spoke back, shrill across the ford: "I am the son of the great knight Raoul of Roche-Bernard, and I will go this way or none, for I would take the cross like him and ride among brave men."

"Get hence," cried he on the horse, "for here you shall not pass. Will I not spurn you from the ford, and you be carried down and lost in this cold stream!"

"I am used to cold and pain," said little Pierre, and stepped out upon the first stone, where the water curled white.

"Stay," cried the old woman, "this is the garment that all who go this way must wear."

And she covered him with the white cloth, so that Count Raoul could see no longer the form of little Pierre, but he thought that his figure had grown to a good, manly height. The swift water twisted the crutch from his hand, for Count Raoul could see it borne down by the stream, but lo, the boy stepped bravely from stone to stone to meet the watcher of the ford.

Then there was darkness, and the drive of mist upon the river, so that he saw nothing more for a time. Yet this too faded at last, and Count Raoul, looking, could behold the far bank of the stream, whereon stood so goodly a band of soldiery he could scarce believe his eyes. Mighty and well-set their charges, silver-bright their arms, and the pennons and emblazonings glowed like the sun. Sure it was sorcery, but there before them on that fair bank stood little Pierre in armor like to theirs, but plain and without a shield. And he was straight in form, and tall—good to look upon.

Then there rode forth to meet him from that company a certain great gentleman of kingly bearing, who wore a crown above the helmet bars, and his face was of one skilled in noble war.

"And who is this," he cried, "that has so boldly crossed the stream into my land?"

"It is little Pierre," said the boy, "son of that great knight Raoul of Roche-Bernard, and I have longed to take the cross like him for the sake of Christ, if ever I could be a knight."

Then cried the other: "Who think you that I am?"

"Nay, I know not, sire," said little Pierre, "but I know that I could love you always, and ride gladly behind your banner, wherever it should lead."

The Token

The great gentleman who wore the crown leaped lightly then from his horse and said: "Shall I make you one of my chivalry?"

Little Pierre answered: "If it please you, sire."

Then spake the other, in a mighty voice: "Kneel, Pierre the Outcast," and he drew his sword. "Lo, you did yearn to take the cross, yet behold, you have borne it all these years. Valiantly have you borne it, nor cried out at the weight thereof. Bold heart have you had, my little child. Truly shall you ride with me, one of my knights without fear, for my heart rejoices in you. Do you know me now?"

"Yes, Lord."

"So rise, Sir Valiant of Roche-Bernard!"

Then Count Raoul saw a banner brought forward, and a blazoned shield—his arms of the Golden Leopard, though so bright he could scarce distinguish them. And all that company gave welcome to Sir Valiant, closing him round, wherefore he could be seen no more.

Pierre the Outcast

Count Raoul beheld the walls of the room beyond the bed, for it was dawn. He sprang to his feet and looked upon the little body before him, but it lay quite still. Only, the face was no longer twisted and worn, but beautiful in the gray light, as of one who has fallen in victory behind his shield. Then he cried out and fell forward, burying his face within the covering of the bed, and his sobbing was piteous to hear.

When little Pierre was buried in the chapel, Count Raoul had him wrapped in cloth of gold, and his tomb set before the very steps of the altar; and thereon the figure as of a knight with the full arms of Roche-Bernard, to which was added a cross and aureole, very fair to see. And he caused the entablature to be thus inscribed: *Here lies Sir Valiant, only son of Raoul. The last of many knights—most honored of them all.*

Here it was that my Lord was wont to pray during the season of Lent until his death, and the stone was worn by his knees.

Lady Blanche

THOMAS, Lord John's son of Sarzeau, married Annette of Roche-Bernard and held the castle and lands in fief by right of kin. He was a brave man and of good fame, so that the domain rejoiced. But after the wedding, Lady Blanche, who had been chatelaine of Roche-Bernard those years since Count Raoul's death, called to her the bride and unclasped the keys from her girdle.

"It is now right, foster daughter, that I, who am old, should stand back for you. Have here the keys of this place in token that my rule is at end. None are withheld."

Then Annette, who knew the heart of her

mother, the pride thereof and her use in government, embraced her. "Sweet lady, no! While you
live, saving my Lord, none shall have voice in
Roche-Bernard."

But for all that, Lady Blanche put the keys in
her hands. "It shall be as I will," she answered.
"My winters are over, and I know that who
strives with time gets only scorn for it. It is your
duty to bear this weight, as I have taught you,
but mine to lay it down."

And thus it was also that she sat no longer in
the high place at board, nor oversaw the work of
the castle, giving way in all things to the Lady
Annette. Less and less the servants turned to her
for command, and old faces among them were
replaced by new, so that, whereas once the name
of my Lady had been upon the lips of all in castle
and field, and her renown was spread through
Brittany, it was no long time before men spoke
of her but rarely.

Once she said to Annette, when they were
alone: "Old Age is a grim schoolmaster, foster

daughter, who clips our pride, showing how small our place is, and quickly filled. I thought only *I* could do some things, but you do them well."

In those days she sat long hours in her room, or looked from the window. Bent she was, and withered. Yet there was worse to come, for on a day she called Annette to her and said: "It is a misty season—this summertime."

"Not so, *ma dame*. It is blue and fine weather."

Then my Lady cried out: "Oh Annette, God is not pitiful to me!"

It was soon thereafter that she was blind.

So the nights and days passed slowly, but because of high courage, she endured all this in silence as became her. Once only, before the fire with Lord Thomas, her brother's son, when he had asked what tidings she had from Sarzeau, "It is hard," she said, "that of those I knew, being young, there is not one alive with whom to speak of yonder days. And I count this loneliness of age most grievous of all."

Lady Blanche

Annette sat much with her talking, or asked counsel touching household matters, for this Lady Blanche liked best. Nor was it long before they brought to her Annette's firstborn, craving her blessing. Then my Lady felt the child from head to foot, smiling, and said he was a stout boy, well formed, who would bring greatness to Roche-Bernard. But for all their kindliness, she was wont to call this her waiting time.

It was at Christmas in her last year, when there were many fine guests at the castle, that there rode up two gentlemen, asking shelter. One of them was white of beard but richly dressed; the other was young and tall. My Lord Thomas gave them welcome befitting their rank. When they had drunk a cup, he asked who they were that honored him.

The old man answered: "It may be that my name is known to you, as elsewhere in France, for I am Huon of Bordeaux, who was called Le Roy. And this is my scholar."

The Token

When he had heard this, my Lord clasped him in his arms. "Welcome," he said, "you great singer. This is grace indeed that you have come."

Messire Huon answered sadly: *"Beau sire*, I was welcomed once for my voice, when it was a joy to feel music within me. But the years have silenced it. And now my songs live only on the lips of others."

Then my Lady Annette came quickly into the hall and greeted him. When he had spoken seemly words, he said: *"Ma dame,* is it not so that I held you once on my knees, when you were called the Lark of Roche-Bernard?" Then he kissed her on both cheeks and they made much of him, for it was told how he had guested at the castle years before. But men saw that Messire Huon gazed here and there about the hall, and would have spoken.

At last, he said: "Time has taken to himself many fair things, and maybe I had vain hopes— where is my Lady?"

Lord Thomas answered that she lived, but was

life-weary and blind. "Yet when she hears of your coming, I know well it will be joy and strength to her." So they sent word that Huon Le Roy craved audience of Lady Blanche in the hall.

These tidings were brought to her as she sat alone. When the servant boy had spoken, she rose from her chair, trembling. After a moment she asked: "What of Messire Huon? How looks he? Is he beautiful, as of old?"

The boy answered: "He is a stately gentleman."

My Lady turned away, leaning upon the chair. "Tell him I cannot come. I am ill and weak. Bid him welcome from me, but I cannot come." Yet, as the servant was leaving, she cried: "Tell him I will come presently, and bid him loving welcome to Roche-Bernard." Then she called her woman, and bade her seek out a fine dress, but of dark color. She wore also a silver girdle. When all was ready, "It is well," she said, "that I have no longer eyes to look in the mirror, for thus I may fancy myself neither old nor worn." The woman led her down slowly into the hall, but she could feel how my Lady's heart beat fast as they went.

Messire Huon saw them enter. The knuckles of his sword hand grew white upon the hilt, and he bowed his head. Then he went forward and knelt before her.

"My Lady," he said only, "my Lady!"

She sought his hands, and held them. *"Beau sire,* you have come late; but God has given me this joy, that I may greet you again. Only, Messire Huon, of your great courtesy, I will that you see me rather in remembrance than as I am."

He answered: "I see only the brightness of this honor. And, sweet my Lady, if I come late, know well that your memory has never swerved from my love."

Those who stood by smiled among themselves, that two people grown old should speak so tenderly, and afterward they gathered about Sir Hugh, the younger singer, who made sport for them with new-fashioned rhymes and madrigals. But Lady Blanche and Messire Huon talked long together.

She said: "Your fame has grown brighter with the years, my friend, and your songs are heard everywhere—good songs of noble manners and true living."

"They are less honored of the people now," he answered, "for times are changed; but there are still those that sing them, and a few will not die."

"Tell me," she asked, "did you return to her you told me of so long ago—that girl at the door of the hostelry?"

"I did not return to those ways," he said. "What nobleness in my art there is, and truth, is because of this and you."

The boards were brought in, and a good feast held in honor of these great *trouvères*. Messire Huon sat by Lady Blanche and men gave him due regard, but it was plain to see they listened rather to the jesting of Sir Hugh. He was strong and bold, merry, and of fine bearing, so that women were glad when he turned to them and all laughed at his words. Messire Huon looked on, half smiling. When all had taken their fill, they gathered before the great fire and piled high the logs, for there was winter without, and a keen wind.

Then my Lord Thomas spoke for the rest and said: "Give us of your skill, Messire Huon, if we may ask so far. You have been called the voice of France."

The good minstrel rose and whispered to him.

"That voice is old," he answered aloud, "but you shall hear its echo. It is *The Lay of the Oriflamme*." Then Sir Hugh took up his lute, and Messire Huon made a sign that none should tell my Lady it was not he who sang.

That great verse held sway in the hall: How Love and Honor were rivals for a white rose, high-growing. And the words of Love were like soft fire rising from the lute, but when Honor spoke, it was the ring of a sword. They strove before her in a garden, and Love was slain, nor

gained one of her petals; but the other plucked and wore her, making thereof the blazon of an oriflamme, sacred to Honor among noble hearts.

My Lady listened with parted lips while the others gazed at her, knowing that she was the rose who had been so fair and loved. And there were tears upon the cheeks of many. They looked in wonder at her face, which seemed young again.

Thus the song ended. It was quiet about the fire, for none would be first to break that magic.

At last my Lord Thomas spoke. "We know now the meaning of your greatness, Huon Le Roy, and I do not think that voice of France will be ever silent."

But Messire Huon took the hand of my Lady. "Did it please you?" he said.

She answered: "Only in one thing it displeased me, dear singer. Love was not slain in the garden."

Then many pressed about him with words of praise, but he laughed them off. Much was spoken of the making of songs and the skill therein. And of a sudden, Messire Huon spoke. "Answer me this riddle, my lords and ladies: Which is nobler of the two—great art, or great life which inspires it?"

Some answered this, some that; but after a time, Lady Annette said: "Nay, *beau sire,* of the two, a noble life is finer than fine art, for therein God is the poet."

He said: "You have answered right. And I hold that no skill of singer may win untarnished praise save that, like a vine, it lift itself upon a noble theme. Can art transform the base, or make true a lie? You praise that song—praise her rather who was the soul of it, or better still, praise both, and match them, younger folk, if you can. But I would gladly see you overpass us by reason of them."

There was much said of former times. My Lady Blanche and Messire Huon told gladly of those men they had known, and the others listened, as was fitting. At last Huon Le Roy smiled, pointing at the fire. "There is need of new fagots," he said, "for the first are burned down. We will leave you to kindle them." He took my Lady's hand, while those who were there showed them due reverence.

So they passed together out from the lighted hall. And when fresh logs were brought and the fire burned high, men talked of them both for a while.